Slap

by Alexis Gregory

TEAM
ANGELICA

Published September 2015 by Team Angelica Publishing,
an imprint of Angelica Entertainments Ltd

Team Angelica Publishing
51 Coningham Road
London W12 8BS

TEAM
ANGELICA

www.teamangelica.com

A CIP catalogue record for this book is available from
the British Library

ISBN 978-0-9569719-8-2

Printed and bound by Lightning Source

Credits:

Written by Alexis Gregory

Directed and designed by Rikki Beadle-Blair.

Cast:

Danny: Frankie Fitzgerald
John: Nigel Fairs
Dominique: Alexis Gregory

Stage Manager: Marie Costa

Make Up Designer: Benjamin Ip

Dramaturg: John Gordon

Developed through the Angelic Tales New Writing Festival

Produced by Rikki Beadle-Blair for Team Angelica and Alexis Gregory for Exact Content

In association with Theatre Royal Stratford East

PR by Kevin Wilson Public Relations

Cover design by ngdesign

Cover photograph by Jane Hobson

One of the first pieces of my own writing I ever performed was at Rikki Beadle-Blair's 50th birthday party at The Drill Hall. The piece was called *Through The Wilderness* and it was about a Madonna-obsessed child growing up in North West London in the 1980s (not even vaguely autobiographical). My five minute piece of 'stand up theatre' was well received and gave me the confidence to continue to explore my voice as a writer. This led to me creating a piece for Rikki and John Gordon's Angelic Tales festival of new plays here at this legendary home of new writing, Theatre Royal Stratford East, a theatre that has always striven to give unheard voices a platform. The title for this new play came to me straight away and I was off.

I wrote *Slap* to explore and highlight a scene I was part of yet also viewing from a distance. I wanted it to be a truth-filled fantasy, an exploration of several themes that fascinate me including sexuality, gender, family, addiction, childhood, the club scene, identity and the intoxicating power of good old fashioned glamour.

It has been an incredible journey for me creating this piece, from starting out writing alone in my bedroom, wondering if anyone would ever be interested in what I had to say, through Angelic Tales; the surprise offer of the play going on to be performed at Channel 4; returning to Stratford East last year to explore the immersive possibilities of how to stage the play in a series of workshop performances, refining and developing it further throughout this process; and now to this current run in the theatre's exciting new space.

I don't know what the next step of the *Slap* journey is but I am thrilled that you are here now sharing this part of it with me. The audiences have been integral to this play's journey and have supported it throughout. Thank you from me... and Dominique.

Alexis Gregory

September 2015

Alexis Gregory would like to thank:

The Actors Centre
Arts Council England
Carleen Beadle
Sarah Buik
Paul Burston
Patrick Cash
Channel 4
Colin Campbell Austin
Robert Chevara
Allison Edwards
Karen Fisher
James Hadley
Jane Hobson
Miss Kimberley
Jay Barry Matthews
Kerry Michael
Ricky Parr
Andrew Piper
Dee-Dee Samuels
David Stuart

All at Theatre Royal Stratford East
Michael Warburton

My family and friends for their support.

I also really want to thank my director, Rikki Beadle-Blair, who has mentored me throughout this process, working tirelessly with me on the play and believing in it since its initial conception. I beyond 'safe word' you.

Director/designer

Rikki Beadle-Blair

Named several years running on the Independent on Sunday's Rainbow List as one the 100 most influential gay people in Britain, Rikki has a life-long commitment to creating challenging, transformative entertainment in the mediums of Film, Theatre, Music, Television, Radio, Dance and Design. He created the production company Team Angelica to pursue these goals and share opportunities with performers, artists and practitioners from the widest possible range of backgrounds.

Rikki wrote *Stonewall* for BBC Films. Directed by Nigel Finch, *Stonewall* went on to win the audience awards at the

London Film Festival and the San Francisco Lesbian and Gay film festival as well an award for Rikki at Outfest LA for Outstanding Screenwriting.

Among other television projects, Rikki wrote, directed and featured in the internationally successful Channel 4 series *Metrosexuality*, also composing the soundtrack.

His radio documentary, *The Roots of Homophobia,* was awarded the Sony Award for Best Documentary Feature.

He was a writer and the executive story editor for the US TV series *Noah's Arc*, and was supervising director of debut films with first-time gay filmmakers as a director for the 'Out in Africa' organization in South Africa.

Rikki's short film *Souljah*, about a transgendered West African child-soldier, won best film at the Rushes London Short film festival.

Rikki has directed four successful independent feature films for his company Team Angelica: *Fit* and *Free*, about young sexuality and homophobic bullying – both films were distributed to every school in the UK and have become a phenomenon with screenings world-wide; *KickOff*, a comedy about a football match between a gay and straight football team; and the film version of his hit play *Bashment*, set in the word of homophobic hip-hop/ragga music; He has since then made several more short films, including *Gently*, *7 Dials*, *Thrive*, *Alive*; and *Butterfly*, commissioned by the Royal Albert Hall.

Rikki's theatre work is extensive – personally creating 18

new plays in the last six years, including *Twothousandand-Sex*, the live version of *Stonewall*, plus *Bashment*, *Family-man*, *Shalom Baby* and *Gutted*. His new musical *Bromantics* previews in London in autumn 2015, and will be swiftly followed by his new play, *Elemental*.

Cast (in alphabetical order)

Nigel Fairs

Nigel Fairs trained at Bretton Hall. As an actor, his recent roles include Inspector Morse in *House of Ghosts* (Baroque Theatre Co), Dr Watson in *To Kill a Canary* (Henley), Episcopalian dentist Martyn in *The House* (So and So, London), Douglas, Leonard and Elaine in a one man show *Didn't you used to be Derek Jacobi?* (tour), John George Haigh in his own award-winning play *In Conversation with an Acid Bath Murderer*, and Gavin in another award-winner, *My Gay Best Friend* (co-written and performed with Louise Jameson). Other favourites include Oscar Wilde in *In Extremis* (Kean Productions), Frank Churchill in *Emma*, Noel Coward in *Two Flats and a Sharp* (both Classic Reaction) and Christopher Wren in *The Mousetrap* (West End).

As a writer, Nigel has had more stage plays than Shakespeare produced, seven musicals, over fifty murder mystery scripts and audio serials for *Doctor Who, Sapphire & Steel*, *Blake's Seven* and *The Tomorrow People* (for Big Finish Productions). His latest play, *Driving me Round The Bend* (also co-written with Louise Jameson) premiered at this year's Sevenoaks Festival in June.

Frankie Fitzgerald

Frankie can mostly recently be seen playing Jack Dickson along-side Tom Hardy in *Legend*.

Theatre Credits include: *Gutted* (TRSE) directed by Rikki Beadle-Blair, *Pools Paradise* (UK TOUR) *A Midsummer Night's Dream* for Millpond Media.

Television Credits Include: *Casualty* (BBC), *London Irish* (Channel Four) *The Impressions Show* (BBC) *He Kills Coppers* (ITV) *Holby City* (BBC) *Hotel Babylon* (BBC) *Dream Team* (Sky One) *The Step Father* (ITV) *Eastenders* (BBC)

Film credits include *Strings* (Short) *A London Love Story* (Short) and features *Stormhouse* and *Troy*.

Frankie also runs a number of performing arts schools for children across South London and Kent

www.centrestagetheatreacademy.com.

Alexis Gregory

Slap is Alexis Gregory's debut play as a writer. It was initially developed at Theatre Royal Stratford East's Angelic Tales Festival and then staged at Channel 4 as the first-ever theatrical presentation in the channel's history. His second play, *Bright Skin Light*, has received workshop productions at Stratford East and his third, the verbatim piece *Safe*, based on his interviews with homeless and at-risk LGBT youth, created in association with the Albert Kennedy Trust, has been performed at the Soho Theatre as part of the Pride in London arts festival. Alexis has also written and directed a short film for the Albert Kennedy Trust. Both *Bright Skin Light* and *Safe* return for full runs in 2016, with *Safe*'s development being filmed for a feature length documentary. Alexis is currently developing his forth play *And Where There Once Were Two,* as well as a TV project and a screen adaption of *Slap*. Additional writing includes the short plays *Freak* (Bush Theatre) and *Feast* (Gillette Square Studios, directed by Alexis) and the pub-lished short story 'My Own Private Narcissist'. Alexis has read from his work at the Polari Literary Salon at the Southbank Centre and on the 2014 and upcoming 2015 Polari tours, and he was nominated for an *Out in the City* magazine award in the Rising Star category. Alexis also has his own production company, Exact Content.

Alexis' theatre credits as an actor include *Eight* (Kings Head, Tara Arts, Tristan Bates), *First Signs* (Kings Head), *Sparkle-*

shark ('Write To Play with Phillip Ridley', Southwark Playhouse), Larry Kramer's *A Minor Dark Age* (Operating Theatre Company), *You Couldn't Make It Up* (New End Theatre), workshop productions of *Children At Play* (Young Vic) and *A Thousand Miles of History* (High Tide), and performance art piece *Gasping Words* (ICA); and several plays with Rikki Beadle-Blair's Team Angelica company including *Bashment* (Birmingham Rep), *Kick Off* (Riverside Studios), *Stonewall* (Pleasance Theatres London, Edinburgh Festival and The Drill Hall), and several additional plays with the company at the Tristan Bates Theatre. Screen credits include several of Team Angelicas features films, including *Bashment*, *KickOff*, *Fit* and its follow-up *Free* (*Fit* and *Free* co-produced with Stonewall). Alexis also appeared in the shorts *No Ordinary Joe* and *Road To Damascus* and TV credits include *Casualty* (BBC) and *The Bill* (ITV).

Alexis Gregory

Cast

DOMINIQUE: In her twenties to thirties, trans, glam but tarnished.

DANNY: In his twenties, gay, working class, troubled, a drug dealer running his empire from his bath.

JOHN: In his forties to fifties, a doctor, heterosexual, middle class, educated.

Setting

DOMINIQUE's open-plan bedsit. In the main living area a bed, a sofa and coffee table (with, amongst other objects, a landline placed on it) and then a small bathroom with a bath and a toilet in it.

DOMINIQUE sits on the edge of the bed, waiting; edgy, wired and unable to speak.

We see DANNY in the bathroom (as we do throughout the whole of the play) sitting in the bath, lost in his own world, smoking crystal meth.

After a moment:

DOMINIQUE: *(Mobile phone in hand, pressed to her chest)* C'mon sweetheart. Spit. It. Out. *(Lifts phone and speaks into it. Phone voice)* What's your name darling?...okay, Jeremy, well I really don't wanna rush ya *(Off phone, in her own voice)* but hurry the fuck up. *(On phone. Phone voice)* I offer a full unhurried service. Your pleasure is my pleasure. My measurements are 34/24/34... 8... Yes Jeremy, I am pre op... No Jeremy, I understand... You saw my picture online? ...Well thank you Jeremy. You know being this beautiful used to scare the fuck outta me but some things you get used to. In calls, one hundred and twenty pounds; out calls, one hundred and sixty... You want something 'special'? Look, I don't do shit, piss or bareback, ok?... Oh no, that's fine, you shoulda said... No, don't worry, there'll be no bruising, visible at least. My name? Dominique with a 'q'. Our names are always Dominique or Rachelle or Terri with an 'I'. A Terri with a 'Y' wouldn't last two minutes in my world believe me. *(Jeremy hangs up).* Hello? Jeremy? *(Own voice)* Timewaster. I shoulda known.

DOMINIQUE's second mobile phone rings. She looks at the caller ID, braces herself and then picks up and answers as if she doesn't recognise the number.

DOMINIQUE: Hello?

Lights up on JOHN in a restaurant. The following dialogue is frantic and one line carries on from the next.

JOHN: Dominique. It's John.

DOMINIQUE: John? Hi.

DANNY: Dominique!

DOMINIQUE: Danny?

JOHN: I booked us that table. I'm at that restaurant.

DANNY: DOMINIQUE!

DOMINIQUE: *(To DANNY)* Yes Danny *(To JOHN)* Sorry John?

JOHN: Three hours I've been here. You're with someone.

DANNY: Dominique?

DOMINIQUE: Yes Danny. Yes John, I'm with someone.

JOHN: Well finish up. I'm coming to collect you. I booked you last week.

DANNY: Dominique?

JOHN: Dominique?

DANNY / JOHN: Dominique. Can you hear me?

DOMINIQUE: Oh yeah. I hear ya's.

DANNY / JOHN: Good.

DOMINIQUE: Danny, one second. John, it's a really bad line. *(Moving phone away from her mouth)* Sorry. I'm losing you.

DOMINIQUE throws the phone against the wall. It smashes.

JOHN: Dominique. Hello? *(No response)* Bloody hell.

Lights down on JOHN.

3

DOMINIQUE: Danny baby? Are ya there?

DOMINIQUE heads towards the bathroom. She speaks through the door.

DOMINIQUE: Here we are again. Talking through doors. Like that night you turned up on my doorstep.

Flashback. DANNY bangs on the door. Wild and drug fucked.

DANNY: Dominique. It's me. Open up.

DOMINIQUE: Who's 'me'?

DANNY: Danny.

DOMINIQUE: From the other night?

DANNY: Yeah.

DOMINIQUE starts to head towards the front door.

DOMINIQUE: Brown hair?

DANNY: Yeah.

DOMINIQUE: Blue eyes?

DANNY: Yeah.

DOMINIQUE: Cute?

DANNY: Definitely yeah.

4

DOMINIQUE: I'm sorry. I don't remember ya.

DOMINIQUE heads back to the bed.

Back to the present day.

DANNY: Fuck, you made me work for it.

DOMINIQUE: I'm worth it though.

DANNY: So am I.

Flashback.

DANNY pounds on the door again. DOMINIQUE heads back to the front door.

DANNY: How can you not remember me?

DOMINIQUE: I just don't.

DANNY: Tryin' to forget me are ya? Easier said than done.

DOMINIQUE: Oh I'm saying Danny and I'm doing Danny. Good night Danny.

DANNY: Come off it Dominique. Let a geezer in yeah. We only just got started.

DOMINIQUE: Just got started? You were here for three days. We were only supposed to be sharing a cab back from Treacles but you couldn't control yourself. I thought the driver was gonna chuck us out but you said...

DANNY: "You can't chuck us out here. Anything could happen. Look at this shit-hole" and you said...

DOMINIQUE: "Excuse me Danny this is where I live thank you" and as soon as we hit the pavement...

DANNY vomits.

DANNY: ...all down your dress and you said...

DOMINIQUE: *(Reacting to DANNY's vomit all down her)* "Couldn't you have done it in the bloody cab Danny?" I'd never seen anyone so wild-eyed and scared... until later, because anything and everything did happen.

DANNY: Don't tell me you didn't enjoy it.

DOMINIQUE: I won't.

DANNY: Bet you thought you wouldn't see me again. I ain't one of your punters.

DOMINIQUE: I know.

DANNY: And I ain't like any of those other boys.

DOMINIQUE: Oh, I know, but you're gay Danny; into men and that ain't me. I thought your temporary dalliance with the fairer sex, that *is* me, was just that; temporary.

DANNY: I wanna make it something more permanent.

DOMINIQUE: Like an unsightly scar or misspelt tattoo?

DANNY: Like Niagara Falls, the Great Wall of China or the Pyramids. Like one of the great wonders of the world; unmoveable and eternal, radiating and visible from outta space.

DOMINIQUE: Go home Danny.

DOMINIQUE sits back down on the bed.

DANNY: You know I don't normally do this kinda thing yeah, rocking up at someone's doorstep at... at...

DOMINIQUE: It's 5 a.m. Danny and I got news for you. I don't do this either. I ain't your experiment, your kink, your fetish or ya dirty secret.

DANNY: Fine. I'll be yours. Open up. I wanna play with ya.

DOMINIQUE: I ain't no Scalextric.

DANNY: I was thinking more Barbie doll.

DOMINIQUE: Fuck Barbie and while ya at it fuck Ken too. Good night Danny.

DANNY: Fuck 'em both? Now ya talking. When I was a kid I'd play with Action Man. I couldn't play with Barbie. I was too scared 'cause boys don't play with dolls. I remember peeping down the front of my Action Man's combats, checking him out, hoping for a dick like mine cause two's company, but no, nothing apart from a bump. A plastic mound. I always wondered if Barbie was packing and hiding something like what I had but I never got to find out.

DOMINIQUE: So you're looking for a Barbie doll with a dick. Now there's a Special Feature Limited Edition. If you find one of those you better hold onto it.

DANNY: I plan to. Wanna be my Barbie?

DOMINIQUE: I'm less Barbie more She Ra. She kicks more ass.

DANNY: Gangsta. You can be my She Ra and I'll be your He Man and we can fight the evil forces together.

DOMINIQUE: Ain't a pretty boy like you got a boyfriend, shag or insignificant other to take on the world with?

DANNY: Rather do it with you. I know I ain't supposed to be getting down with...

DOMINIQUE: ...with?...

DANNY: ...my future wife but...

DOMINIQUE: *(Interrupting)* 'Future wife'? Rushing me up the aisle already are ya Danny? Don't worry, you ain't got me up the duff or nothing.

DANNY: I know I ain't... yet... but the night is young... yeah.

DOMINIQUE heads towards the door.

DOMINIQUE: Well wouldn't that be a miracle of modern science eh Danny?

DOMINIQUE opens the front door.

DANNY: Yeah babe, to add to an already existing miracle of modern nature.

DANNY is violently sick down DOMINIQUE's dress.

Back to present day.

DOMINIQUE: Danny. My Danny. One disaster after another with you. They call you Titanic 'cause you got a habit of taking everyone down with ya. Not me though. We're gonna prove them wrong ain't that right Danny? Danny?

DANNY: What's that babe?

DOMINIQUE: You and me babe. Proving 'em all wrong babe.

DANNY: Innit babe.

DOMINIQUE: Open up then. You've been in that bath forever. I thought you'd fallen asleep.

DANNY: Nah babe. I'll sleep when I'm dead.

DOMINIQUE: I doubt it. Come on. Open up. I've almost forgotten what ya look like.

DANNY looks in the mirror. Wired and tripping over own reflection.

DANNY: Like everything you ever wished I'd be. Like everything I am and like everything I'll always be. I'm your pin up, your ideal man, your bad boy, your very own James Dean, Marlon Brando and Paul Newman.

DOMINIQUE: I like the sound of you.

DANNY: I like the sound of you too.

DOMINIQUE: 'Like' like or 'like' like?

DANNY: 'Like' like.

DOMINIQUE: Well that clarifies that then. Open up babe. Spend some time with me.

DANNY: I will.

DOMINIQUE: I'm waiting Danny.

DANNY: One minute babe.

DOMINIQUE: A little less conversation a little more action Danny. Do something babe, anything. If ya cared about me you would...

DANNY: I do care.

DOMINIQUE: Do ya? How much? This much? *(She opens her arms)* Or this much? *(She opens her arms wider)*

DANNY: This much babe.

DANNY kneels down at the bathroom door, smokes some more crystal and then blows the smoke through the keyhole. DOMINIQUE sees the smoke emerge and kneels down on the other side of the door. DANNY blows some more smoke through. DOMINIQUE inhales.

DOMINIQUE: I'm still not sure babe.

*DANNY blows more smoke through the keyhole.
DOMINIQUE inhales.*

DOMINIQUE: Oh, I get it. That much.

A knock on the door. DOMINIQUE and DANNY scream.

DANNY: Who the fuck is it?

DOMINIQUE: Wait there babe.

DANNY: Who is it?

*DOMINIQUE goes to the door and then tentatively looks
through the peephole. It is JOHN. DOMINIQUE is wired
now.*

DOMINIQUE: It's some geezer.

DANNY: Don't let him in.

DOMINIQUE: It's okay. I can handle him.

DANNY: You know him?

DOMINIQUE: No. Yes. No.

DANNY: Yes or no?

DOMINIQUE: Yes. I know him.

DOMINIQUE opens the door.

DOMINIQUE: Alright darling?

JOHN: No I'm not. I booked us that table. I was waiting. I thought that's what we were doing tonight but you're… here… as am I… hi… Right, there's a taxi waiting outside. They're holding us that table. I'm taking you out. Are you ready or shall I wait in here?

JOHN moves to head through the door. DOMINIQUE steps in front of him.

DOMINIQUE: Not now darlin'. I got a guest. Now what did we agree?

JOHN: 'No privileges and no queue jumping'. Ok, I'll wait outside. As we agreed Dominique… as you please, Dominique.

JOHN turns around to go but stops and turns back.

JOHN: Tonight will be special. I've decided. For both of us. But later… yes, later.

The landline rings.

JOHN: I'll get that.

JOHN goes to step into the flat again. DOMINIQUE stops him again.

DOMINIQUE: No ya won't.

JOHN: I'd like to.

DOMINIQUE: I know you'd like to but I said no.

JOHN: Yes you did didn't you Dominique but are you sure Dominique?

JOHN goes to step in the flat again. DOMINIQUE stops him.

DOMINIQUE: John, you know what happens when I have to repeat myself.

JOHN smiles to himself at the memory of being punished by DOMINIQUE.

JOHN: Yes I do Dominique. Tell me again please Dominique.

DOMINIQUE: No! Enough! And that bloody phone'll stop ringing. They tend to do that.

DOMINIQUE and JOHN stand staring at each other waiting for the phone to stop ringing. It doesn't. Finally it does.

DOMINIQUE: There. See?

JOHN: Indeed. You're always right Dominique. Bloody women. Thank you Dominique. Thank you.

JOHN smiles at her and then suddenly scurries away. DOMINIQUE calls after JOHN.

DOMINIQUE: I should be bloody charging for this!

DOMINIQUE returns to the flat and heads towards the

bathroom door.

DOMINIQUE: Danny?

DANNY: Has he gone?

DOMINIQUE: Yes he's gone. You can open up now.

DANNY: I'm fine in here.

DOMINIQUE: I'm sure you are Danny but I'd prefer to talk to you rather than a wooden door.

DANNY: Who was it?

DOMINIQUE: No one. A punter.

DANNY: No one or a punter?

DOMINIQUE: Both.

DANNY: And?

DOMINIQUE: And I got rid of him.

DANNY: Good... cause I woulda been out there if there was any trouble Dominique. He wouldn't wanna fuck with me Dominique... you hear me Dominique?

DOMINIQUE: I know Danny.

DOMINIQUE sits on the bed.

DANNY: You're still doin' that then?

DOMINIQUE: Yes.

DANNY: Don't you find it humiliating?

DOMINIQUE: No more so than life itself.

DANNY: I worry 'bout ya.

DOMINIQUE: No need. You know Danny, to be in this game and not get fucked up by it you either gotta be incredibly smart or incredibly stupid. Well I was always top of the class Danny. Anyway, what else can I do? Who else will have me?

DANNY: I'll have you.

DOMINIQUE: Well open up then.

DANNY lights up his pipe and inhales heavily.

DANNY: That's what I am doin' babe. Right babe. I'm just gonna get back in the bath.

DOMINIQUE heads over to the bathroom door.

DOMINIQUE: Again? You're constantly in and out of that bath.

DANNY: Am I?

DOMINIQUE: You've had six baths already today.

DANNY: Six baths? Today?

DOMINIQUE: You've got no idea have ya? Do you even know what day and what time it is Danny?

DANNY: Of course I do.

DOMINIQUE: Go on then. What day and what time is it Danny?

No answer from DANNY.

DOMINIQUE: What day and what time is it Danny?

DANNY: Is this a trick question?

DOMINIQUE: Of course it fucking ain't. Now answer the fucking question.

A beat.

DANNY: It's today and it's right now and that's all we need to know babe.

A moment – DANNY realises he has no grip on reality. DOMINIQUE realises the same.

DANNY: I'm gonna have that bath.

DOMINIQUE heads back to the bed. DANNY starts muttering to the walls in the bathroom, lost in his own world.

DOMINIQUE: Danny? Who are you talking to in there babe?

DANNY: Me babe? No one babe.

DOMINIQUE: I can hear you muttering 'bout needing someone. Whoever it is you must be talking about me, babe, right babe?

DANNY: Right babe. How'd ya know babe?

DOMINIQUE: Woman's intuition, babe. Make sure you send my love to your imaginary friend, Danny. Tell him he's very welcome to come for tea one day.

DANNY: He's not my imaginary friend babe. But we do talk though. About things, my feelings like.

DOMINIQUE: A bloke talkin' bout his feelings? Very metrosexual. You'll be borrowing my foundation next.

DANNY: Yeah if I feel like re-grouting these tiles in here with it.

DOMINIQUE: Shut it. Maybe I should start chatting to walls, Danny. I'd get more sense outta them than I would outta you.

DANNY: Maybe you would.

DOMINIQUE: Well I hope you and your imaginary friend are very happy together. When you're ready to join your girlfriend in the real world I'll be out here watching TV. Crimewatch is about to start. I'll give ya a shout if you're on it again babe.

DANNY: Thanks babe. But I told ya, he's not my imaginary

friend you know.

DOMINIQUE: Who is it then?

DANNY: My dad.

DOMINIQUE: Ya dad? I've never heard you talk 'bout him
before.

DANNY: He left us Christmas Eve 1988. Mum tried to carry
on as normal. She filled my stocking that night and ate
the mince pies I left out for Santa. Next day she put the
Christmas dinner in and set three places at the table
'cept when it was ready she couldn't take the turkey out
the oven. Couldn't have just two of us at the table. I sat
there on the kitchen floor, close up to the oven like how
I'd watch TV as a kid. My little legs crossed. Front row
seats as our dinner burnt and charred and shrivelled
away to nothing. I hate Christmas now. Worst day of the
year. I'd always done everything with my dad. It was him
who got me into it you know; the dealing. I was seven
years old, ferryin' the gear round the estate in my He
Man lunchbox. Then later he'd get me to mule the E's
into the social club but that was when I was more grown
up, like nine years old. No one woulda thought. I had
such an innocent face.

DOMINIQUE: Still do.

DANNY: Went to my first gay club for my dad. Selling for
him, week after week. "Do this for me Danny. Money's
money. Don't matter where it comes from. It's dirty the
moment it leaves the press". Dad loved the gays though.
He weren't stupid. They were some of his best custom-

ers. I learnt to love 'em too. I better stop now. I might get misty-eyed.

DOMINIQUE: I guess the family that plays together...

DANNY: ...don't stay together. Not us anyway. Dad owed his boss, Mr Diamonds, money. The heavies were sent round to his new place just on the other side of the estate, not that we ever saw him. He tried to escape out the bathroom window but he slipped, fell, landed on a wheelie bin, bounced back off and broke his neck, the stupid cunt. I remember seeing him like that. I was on the way back from the drug run – I'd kept it up as a sign of respect – and there he was, splayed out in the street like a crushed up packet of Twiglets outta the supermarket 'Reduced to Clear' section, a crowd swarming round him. I pushed to the front. I didn't think I would ever see anything worse than that burnt-out Christmas dinner but I was wrong. I was eleven years old. Dad was in a coma for eighteen months. They asked my mum if they should turn the machine off but she said no, that she wanted him to suffer like us. She was fair like that. Till I lost my mum and then...

DOMINIQUE: And then?

DANNY: No more suffering. We'd all had enough of it by then. I had the machine switched off and so here I am. Inherited the family business and my dad's drug debt too. Diamonds weren't going to let us off the hook that easy.

DOMINIQUE: So what does ya Dad say to ya in there Danny?

19

DANNY: Ain't so much 'bout what he says to me babe...it's 'bout what I say to him. I tell him stuff. Like things about when I was little, when I was growing up, things we did together and the things he later missed out on. I tell him about you Dominique, about us, about how I love...

DOMINIQUE: Danny is that your dad I can hear? He's calling you back.

DANNY: Is he? Oh yeah. He is isn't he. Thanks Dominique.

DANNY returns to his conversation with his father. There is an immediate knock on the door.

DOMINIQUE: Fuck (*DOMINIQUE starts to rush over to the door*) Fuck, fuck, fuck, fuck, fuck.

DOMINIQUE opens the door. JOHN is standing there with flowers.

JOHN: Cab's waiting.

DOMINIQUE: Oh for fuck's sake.

DOMINIQUE slams the door in JOHN's face and starts to rush over to the bathroom.

DOMINIQUE: Fuck, fuck, fuck, fuck, fuck.

DOMINIQUE is now at the bathroom door.

DOMINIQUE: Danny (*She caresses the door*) I need some gear.

20

DANNY: That's a bit of a problem you see I ain't got none left.

DOMINIQUE: What about the stuff you're selling? Take from that and we'll replace it.

DANNY: Ain't got none of that either. Musta picked up less than I thought.

DOMINIQUE: Or guzzled it, Greedy Chops.

DANNY: You could go and get some. From the boss. From Diamonds.

DOMINIQUE: I ain't gonna go. You're the man. You go.

From outside:

JOHN: Dominique?

DOMINIQUE looks towards where the voice is coming from. She has an idea.

DOMINIQUE: One second Danny.

DOMINIQUE crossed to the door, opens it and smiles welcomingly at JOHN.

DOMINIQUE: John, darlin'…

JOHN: You done with him yet?

DOMINIQUE: Not yet but I need you to do me a little favour John.

JOHN: *(Flirting)* And how may I be of assistance?

DOMINIQUE: Not like that. Well, like that, but later. You see I need you to go collect something, I'll text ya the address. Go there, pick it up, come back, simple.

JOHN: I thought tonight would be about us.

DOMINIQUE: And it... could be. *(DOMINIQUE starts to bundle JOHN out the flat)* So ya got ya cab downstairs... ya just gotta go to...

JOHN: What is it Dominique?

DOMINIQUE: Sorry?

JOHN: What is it you want me to collect?

DOMINIQUE: John, are you questioning me?

JOHN starts to enjoy receiving this kind of attention from DOMINIQUE – as he always does.

JOHN: No Dominique... but what is it Dominique?

DOMINIQUE: It's girly things, okay John, girly things.

JOHN: What kind of girly things? Something soft?

DOMINIQUE: Nothing soft 'bout me darlin' no matter how hard I try. They're hormone tablets, alright John, there's a guy on the estate that sorts me out, alright John.

JOHN: Hormone tablets aren't particularly girly, Dominique.

DOMINIQUE: They are when they're full of that much oestrogen darling so do us a little favour yeah.

DOMINIQUE tries to bundle JOHN out the flat again.

JOHN: Do you need to take more tablets? I like you how you are.

DOMINIQUE: Well I'm afraid I don't, John. I'm a work in progress.

JOHN: And I like how you're progressing.

DOMINIQUE: There you go then. Now be a good boy. He'll be expecting ya. Go there, pick it up, come back, simple.

JOHN physically stands his ground – he doesn't want to go.

DOMINIQUE: Please.

JOHN: 'Please'?

DOMINIQUE: JUST DO IT!

DOMINIQUE starts to bundle JOHN out the door again.

JOHN: Yes Dominique. Whatever you say Dominique. Thank you Dominique.

JOHN suddenly remembers he has the flowers in his hands. He turns back and presents them to DOMINIQUE. She snatches them off him.

DOMINIQUE: Go.

JOHN scurries off. DOMINIQUE heads back into the flat relieved.

DOMINIQUE: Danny?

DANNY: I'm in here babe.

DOMINIQUE: I know you're still in there babe. You gonna open up?

DANNY: What for?

DOMINIQUE: To be with me, Danny.

DANNY: In a bit.

DOMINIQUE: 'In a bit'? Take me out Danny.

DANNY: Out?

DOMINIQUE: Yeah, out Danny. You're my man and I'm your girl. Take me out. On your arm. Show me off to the world or at least your bloody mates to start with.

DANNY: I can't go out. I just can't.

DOMINIQUE: Ashamed of me are you Danny? Worried the world will find out you're not just a Tranny Fucker but a Tranny Lover too.

DANNY: Don't use that word.

DOMINIQUE: Why not? It's what I am. It's what you are.

DANNY: No it ain't. Neither of us and I ain't ashamed of you.

DOMINIQUE: Ashamed of yourself then. Ashamed that you didn't follow that straight gay path.

DANNY: What straight gay path?

DOMINIQUE: The fucking Yellow Brick Road, Danny. What straight gay path do you think I mean? The one 'you boys' are supposed to follow.

DANNY: 'Us boys'?

DOMINIQUE: You gay boys. The path where you end up with a carbon print copy of yourself 'cause it's nicer and neater and safer that way. With ya matching muscles, ya matching tans, ya matching tattoos and ya matching six-packs, tripping and trolling down the Boulevard of Broken Queens to a pumping and throbbing disco beat.

DANNY: Babe. I was never gonna end up with a copy of myself was I? I mean where would I find a bloke that good-looking and don't be hating on us gay boys Dominique. We don't need no in-house fighting. We ain't the enemy.

DOMINIQUE: I know you ain't but I ain't gay and so I ain't part of your house.

DANNY: You could be. You just gotta come on in cause like Sister Sledge once said, 'I got all my sisters with me'. I

25

got my Soho Gay, my Vauxhall Gay, my East End Gay, my Grindr Gay, my Scruff Gay, my Masc Gay, My Femme Gay, My Fat Gay, my Black Gay, my Asian Gay, my Twinky Gay, my Go Go Gay, my Kylie Gay, my Madonna Gay, my Gaga Gay, My Go-Go Gay, my Scene Queen Gay, my Non Scene Gay, my Chill Out Gay, my Scorchio Gay, my Power Gay, my Power Bottom Gay, My Good Gay, My Bad Gay, my Out Gay, my In Gay, my Shake It All About Gay...

DOMINIQUE: Babe. That's a lot of gay.

DANNY: *(Flirty)* Innit babe.

DOMINIQUE: And I ain't any of 'em. So what kinda gay are you Danny?

DANNY: I'm a Dominique kinda gay. I was always drawn to anything that glistened and sparkled. I just can't help myself.

DOMINIQUE: You wanna be careful with that trait. Could get you into trouble.

DANNY: Already has and you don't have to be gay to come play with me. Queer would work too.

DOMINIQUE: I don't like that word babe. It takes me back.

DANNY: Then let it take ya forward. Queer as in different. As in special. As in real...

DOMINIQUE: I'm still not sure. Keep 'em coming.

DANNY: As in hot to trot. As in rebellious. As in kinda… fabulous.. as in… you.

DOMINIQUE: I like it. I'm keeping it.

DANNY: Do it. It's yours. Cause Queer ain't Gay babe. Though if the straightest path you can think of is the Yellow Brick Road than you're gayer than you think. We don't need no Yellow Brick Road babe. We'll make our own road and follow it too and I'll show you off to who-ever I want babe. I ain't like the other boys. Gay or straight. I never was. Bet you weren't neither.

Silence.

DANNY: Sorry.

DOMINIQUE: No. You're right. I wasn't like the other boys… obviously.

DANNY: So what were you like?

DOMINIQUE: I was a little shit. You?

DANNY: I was a little shit too.

DOMINIQUE: Perfect. We was meant to be.

DANNY: You don't talk 'bout it much… your 'before'.

DOMINIQUE: I ain't got no 'before'.

DANNY: Everyone's got a 'before'.

DOMINIQUE: Well I ain't, okay. Anyway, it don't matter now.

DANNY: You're right babe. It don't.

The landline rings.

DANNY: You should get that Dominique.

DOMINIQUE: Nah. I think you should.

DANNY: I mean I would but...

DOMINIQUE: But?

DANNY: But I'm in here and the phone's out there.

DOMINIQUE: Nothing gets past you Danny.

DANNY: Please Dominique. Answer it. For me.

DOMINIQUE: Oh for fuck's sake. But only 'cause you asked so nicely. *(DOMINIQUE remains where she is)* Just going over to it now Danny, as fast as my legs can carry me.

The landline stops ringing.

DOMINIQUE: Oh. It's stopped. Shit. Take me out Danny. Take me to the pub on the estate for fuck's sake. As long as I'm with ya I don't care.

DANNY: I wouldn't take ya down the Royston Arms. You're too good for that dump.

DOMINIQUE: No I ain't. They'd love me down there. They'd love us. We'd be show-stoppers. The karaoke grinding to an immediate halt as we make our entrance. I'd sit in the corner with the girls and swap make up tips and you'd drink beer with the boys. I'd come over occasionally and hang with you and your mates, not so often as to appear needy or insecure but just enough to let you know I care. You'd be the envy of 'em all. They'd understand the importance of a dolly bird on their arm, the value of a trophy wife.

DANNY: Is that what you are – my trophy wife?

DOMINIQUE: I feel more like the booby prize right now Danny. You won't take me here and you won't take me there. Maybe we should stick to the Yellow Brick Road 'cause we're fucked when we try step off it.

DANNY: I'd take you somewhere better than the pub. I'd take you for dinner.

DOMINIQUE: Nice. KFC or Chicken Cottage, Danny?

DANNY: Me mum and dad's. I'd take you back to the house I grew up in. We could have dinner together. Like a proper family again.

DOMINIQUE: Taking me to meet the family? They'll think it's...

DANNY: ...serious? They'd be right.

DOMINIQUE gets up and heads to the bathroom.

DOMINIQUE: Then let's do it. Take me back to where ya came from. Let us exist someplace other than here. Please.

DANNY: I wish I could. But I can't. It's all gone.

DOMINIQUE: Fine. I'll go out alone then.

Music starts to blast out. Stewart Who and Wayne G 'Bitch'. Dominique jumps up on the table – it is now a club podium. She dances, lost in her own world.

DANNY: Dominique, what you doing?

DOMINIQUE: Having fun Danny. Remember that? I'm out babe. In Vauxhall. In the club. With all those boys you were talking about. You're missing out here Danny. It's party time. Woo.

DANNY: You what babe?

DOMINIQUE: It's pumping in here babe. It's going off.

DANNY: Is it?

DOMINIQUE: It's time to shake what my surgeon gave me. It's packed, Danny, all these hunks with their shirts off. She Ra's gonna get herself a new He Man. You're fired.

DOMINIQUE sticks two fingers up in the direction of the bathroom and blows raspberries.

DANNY: Fuck you babe. It's you, yourself and... you. Private party for one is it? Sounds proper lonely.

DOMINIQUE: Nothing private 'bout this party babe and it certainly ain't proper. When the cat's away…

DANNY: Shut up Dominique.

DOMINIQUE: Boys, Danny. Everywhere I look. All hot and sweaty in here and we're all chasing that high; fighting to make this moment last before the sun comes up and we come down… and… ewww… a drag queen… faker… fuck off back to your own clubs… and those boys, Danny… disappearing into the cubicles two by two… Noah would be proud. Maybe I should join 'em in there Danny *(DOMINIQUE jumps down off the podium / bed)* 'cause you know what they say… two's company but three's a party…

DANNY: Stay there. Where I can hear you.

DOMINIQUE: Getting jealous are we Danny?

DANNY: No.

DOMINIQUE: Ya should be. All these men staring at me. Like flies round honey they are.

DANNY: That's enough now Dominique.

DOMINIQUE: Oh I'm just getting started Danny. Now who is that gorgeous guy staring at?

DANNY: Not you Dominique. You're in a fucking gay club. You won't pull in there love. They like their men.

DOMINIQUE heads over to the bathroom door.

31

DOMINIQUE: Security? You wanna search me? You think I've been acting shady? Oh, you have no idea darlin'. Now, I know my rights... I'm entitled to a full strip-search and how about chucking in a complimentary internal. Come on darlin'... do your worst.

DOMINIQUE faces the bathroom door and clings to the door frame, legs parted ready for a body search and about to bend over for the rest. DANNY opens the bathroom door. The music suddenly stops. DOMINIQUE and DANNY are both face to face.

DOMINIQUE: Thank fuck. I have been dying for a pee.

DOMINIQUE pushes DANNY aside and enters the bathroom. DOMINIQUE goes over to the toilet and is about to sit down and pull her knickers down.

DANNY: Don't you want me to turn around then?

DOMINIQUE: You never used to be so considerate.

DANNY: You never used to be so brazen.

Flashback.

DOMINIQUE: Turn around then.

DANNY: What?

DOMINIQUE: I said turn around. I need to pee.

DANNY: And?

DOMINIQUE: And. You need to turn around.

DANNY: It's not like I ain't seen it before. I am very, very familiar with it...

DOMINIQUE: Sssh, Danny, don't talk about 'it' like that.

DANNY: I wanna watch. Do you stand up or sit down?

DOMINIQUE: Danny!

DANNY: When you piss? Do you stand up or sit down?

DOMINIQUE: Depends.

DANNY: On what?

DOMINIQUE: On who's watching and how much they're willing to pay now turn around.

DANNY: No. I wanna watch.

DOMINIQUE: You dirty bastard.

DANNY smiles.

DANNY: Go on. Please.

DOMINIQUE sits down on the loo and starts to pee.

DANNY: Nice. Now stop.

DOMINIQUE: What?

DANNY: Standing up now.

DOMINIQUE: Make your fucking mind up. This ain't fucking multiple choice.

DANNY: Do it.

DOMINIQUE: Oh for fuck's sake.

DOMINIQUE does as she is told. She eventually finishes peeing.

DANNY: Nice.

DOMINIQUE: Happy now? Pervert.

DANNY: Very.

DOMINIQUE: God, you're even more fucked up than I thought.

DANNY: Thanks.

Present day.

DOMINIQUE: I hope you been topping up with hot water or you'll catch ya death.

DANNY: Waiting for you to heat it up ain't I.

DOMINIQUE looks at DANNY for a moment

DANNY: You getting in or what?

DANNY puts his hand out to help DOMINIQUE in – she dips a high-heeled foot in to test the water and then gets in the bath. She sits in front of DANNY who wraps his arms around her.

DOMINIQUE: Wow.

DANNY: So ya get it now?

DOMINIQUE melts into the moment.

DOMINIQUE: You. Me. Here. The warm. What's not to get?

DANNY finds DOMINIQUE's hand and holds it. He then lifts their hands out of the water. DOMINIQUE runs her hand down DANNY's arm.

DOMINIQUE: I could stay here all day.

DOMINIQUE submerges herself under the water.

DANNY: We already have.

DOMINIQUE pops back up.

DOMINIQUE: I've been listening to you.

DANNY: And whadda I say?

DOMINIQUE: You're hungry. Bet they can hear your stomach rumble on the other side of Westfield. When did ya last eat babe?

DANNY: Is this another trick question?

DOMINIQUE: No babe. I'm gonna pop out babe.

DOMINIQUE gets out the bath.

DANNY: No. Stay here.

DOMINIQUE: But babe, the kitchen cupboard is bare. Have we even got a kitchen cupboard?

DANNY: Have we even got a kitchen?

DOMINIQUE: Oh yeah babe, we definitely got a kitchen. I'll be back babe.

DANNY: You can't go out. You're soaking wet.

DOMINIQUE: I'll dry.

DOMINIQUE leaves the flat.

DANNY: What the fuck?

DANNY takes a moment.

DANNY: Dominique? Are ya there? C'mon. We gotta get ready. I'm taking you out. To me mum and dad's for that dinner. The Prodigal Son returning home with his gorgeous new girlfriend. All of us sat at the dinner table. Small talk at first but soon we'll be laughing. Dad'll get drunk. He's proper mental when he's drunk, "Come on Danny let's have another one. We're celebrating." Celebrating what Dad? "Life Danny. Life." Mum'll get drunk too: "I'm glad I got the dinner sorted Danny or else I'd be bloody useless in the kitchen like this." What the fuck, we'll all get drunk. All of us laughing and tucking into my mum's roast dinner with you, the new addition to the family. There'll be beef and potatoes and vegetables and gravy too. Yeah gravy and dessert. A big chocolate cake that kept us coming back for more. Mum would've pulled out all the stops for you. She'd of done me proud. After the meal, you'll help her clear the plates away, you two in the kitchen chatting and laughing, me and Dad still at the dinner table. He'll say that he liked you. That you and I remind him of himself and my mum when they were young. We'll stay over. I'd offer to sleep on the sofa, let you have a bed, but Dad'll say "No. It's cool. Get stuck in there Danny" and you and me will end up in the bedroom I had as a kid. Tucked up tight in my single bed, unable to sleep, high on life and the cheap sugar rush from Mum's bought-in chocolate cake. You hear me Dominique? C'mon Dominique. We're doing it. We're going out.

DANNY begins to submerge himself in his bathwater as JOHN arrives back with a parcel. JOHN shouts through the door.

JOHN: Dominique?

DANNY: *(Pulling himself up out of the water)* What the fuck?

JOHN: Dominique. I'm back. I'm coming in.

DANNY: No you fucking ain't, mate. Fuck off.

JOHN enters the flat.

JOHN: Are you still with… someone? I did as you asked. I got your… you know.

DANNY: No, I don't know. Who the fuck are ya mate? She ain't here. Fuck off. Go on fuck off outta here.

JOHN moves further into the flat.

JOHN: Sir, sorry to interrupt you but your time is up. Whatever it is that you're both doing in there… it's done… it's over… it's my turn. Fair is fair. Dominique, I'll be out here waiting.

DANNY: Fuck off.

JOHN: (*To the punter, i.e. DANNY*) Yes sir, out here waiting. She's clocked off. Finito. Dominique, you're done. I'm here now… John.

DANNY: Well fuck off John or whatever the fuck your name is. Fuck off back to Mayfair or Kensington or wherever the fuck you're from. We're happy here. Happy without you.

JOHN: Yes. John. Me, and I'm taking you out tonight…

DANNY: Taking her out? You fuckin' wish you crazy fuckin'…

DANNY is about to burst out of the bathroom and go for JOHN. At that second DOMINIQUE appears on the landing with a carrier-bag full of shopping. DANNY remains in the bathroom doorway.

DOMINIQUE: DANNY! NO!

JOHN: Dominique. Where have you been?

DOMINIQUE: I was out.

JOHN: You're soaking wet.

DOMINIQUE: Am I?

DANNY: Who the fuck is this guy?

DOMINIQUE: *(To DANNY)* Just another punter.

JOHN: *(Laughing at the absurdity)* A punter? *(DOMINIQUE ushers JOHN away from Daniel)* I'd bloody go somewhere else if this was the service I was receiving. I've got your parcel Dominique.

JOHN produces the package. DOMINIQUE darts back to JOHN, grabs the package and hugs it to her body like a mother reunited with her baby.

DOMINIQUE: Oh thank fuck.

JOHN: Gosh. You must need them badly.

DOMINIQUE: I do. *(DOMINIQUE heads over to the bathroom door and waves the package in front of DANNY's face)* And so the female of the species returns to the male as feeding commences *(DOMINIQUE lobs the package into the bathroom)* in his nest. *(To DANNY)* I'll get rid of him. Trust me. He's just some punter who's obsessed with me. Thinks it's more than it is. Now you stay in there, Danny. Your sanctuary, your place of solitude and comfort.

DANNY: You trying to get rid of me?

DOMINIQUE: Why would I be? It's just that... I got a surprise for you.

DANNY: A surprise. What is it?

DOMINIQUE: Well, it's a... surprise Danny! The clue's in the title.

DANNY: I don't know if I like surprises.

DOMINIQUE: Trust me sweetheart. You'll like this one. I'll give you a shout when it's ready.

DANNY: Just get rid of him yeah.

DANNY scurries back into the bathroom and the drug package.

DOMINIQUE turns her attention to JOHN.

DOMINIQUE: You are my knight in shining armour.

JOHN: And a maiden should always see that her knight is rewarded.

JOHN gestures towards the door.

DOMINIQUE: Yes but not yet.

DOMINIQUE goes to the kitchen to drop off her shopping. JOHN shouts through to her:

JOHN: Pretty hefty parcel there Dominique. Planning on turning the whole estate female?

DOMINIQUE *(Off)*: They should be so bloody lucky.

JOHN starts to head towards the bathroom, he wants to investigate but he is interrupted by DOMINIQUE's return.

DOMINIQUE: Right. Lovely. All under control, just how we like it. Now I'd better tidy up.

JOHN: After your guest?

DANNY: Guest? No! You're the bloody guest mate.

The landline starts to ring. DOMINIQUE and JOHN stop and stare at it. DANNY in the bathroom stops and stares in the phone's direction too.

JOHN: I'll get that bloody phone.

DOMINIQUE / DANNY: No!

JOHN shakes his head, defeated.

JOHN: Okay… well, I have some tidying up of my own to do too.

JOHN heads off to the kitchen.

DANNY: You said you'd get him out Dominique.

DOMINIQUE: I can't Danny. I can't.

JOHN returns carrying some empty bin bags.

JOHN: 'Danny. Danny. Danny'. All I hear is bloody 'Danny, Danny, Danny'. Yes. I am definitely doing the right thing here.

JOHN starts to look around the flat for what he can remove.

JOHN: That bloody phone. Let me just get that...

DOMINIQUE / DANNY: We said no!

DOMINIQUE heads towards JOHN to stop him answering.

JOHN: I'll get it if I want. No more being told what to do.

DOMINIQUE: But you like that John, don't ya John.

JOHN: No I don't, Dominique. I was trying to. For you. I thought it might help but it led us nowhere. Kept us stagnant and rotting. The changes start now Dominique.

JOHN goes to answer the phone but it stops ringing just before he can answer it.

JOHN: Bloody typical. Right. I don't want to do this but I have to. It's time.

JOHN picks up DANNY's He Man lunchbox.

DOMINIQUE: No John. Don't touch the He Man lunchbox.

That's Danny's.

JOHN: Exactly. It has to go.

JOHN holds the lunchbox above the bin bag.

DANNY: You what? Tell him to put that down, Dominique. My dad gave me that when I was a kid, to keep me drugs in.

DOMINIQUE: See, Danny. This punter's crazy, Danny. He comes over, cleans the place, I tell him it looks shit, spit in his face and he does it all over again. He loves it. This geezer's keeping a roof over our heads.

JOHN: Too right I bloody am.

DANNY: Go on then Dominique.

DOMINIQUE: What?

DANNY: Give him what he's paid for.

DOMINIQUE rushes over to JOHN, spits in his face and then backs away again.

DOMINIQUE: There Danny. Happy Danny? I did it Danny.

DANNY: Well done Dominique. That's my girl, Dominique. Comin' round here nickin' my stuff. It's the posh ones you gotta watch.

JOHN wipes the spit off his face.

JOHN: At last. A connection. This is something, Dominique. A shift. A change. I forgive you Dominique. I know this isn't you. I just want the old Dominique back.

DANNY: You don't know the old Dominique, mate! Or the new one neither.

DOMINIQUE: Yeah. You're only meant to be cleaning.

DOMINIQUE rushes over to the bed and pulls the covers off – more mess for JOHN to clean.

DOMINIQUE: C'mon, clean faster ya filthy fuck.

JOHN: Well I didn't expect you to be this much into it but again, this is good, this is better than expected. I'm proud of you Dominique.

DANNY: You got no right to be proud you prick!

JOHN continues to sort through DANNY's stuff but then stops, and turns and stares at DOMINIQUE. DOMINIQUE is swaying on the spot, high and tweaking.

JOHN: Tell me Dominique. What drugs are you taking?

DOMINIQUE: Drugs? Me?

JOHN: You said you stopped all that when Danny... you need help Dominique.

DOMINIQUE goes to head off to the kitchen.

DOMINIQUE: We all need help John.

44

JOHN chases after DOMINIQUE and grabs her by the arm.

JOHN: Let me help you. Let me be the one. I don't like to see you like this Dominique. I can't help that I care about you. You're my girlfriend.

DANNY: Girlfriend?

DOMINIQUE: See, Danny, crazy, Danny and ssssh, John please.

JOHN: No I will not 'sssssh'. Why should I? I didn't want to do it like this. This is why I booked that table for us. I have something to tell you...

DOMINIQUE: Oh dear god please don't tell me that you were really born a woman. I don't think I can take that right now...

JOHN gets down on one knee.

DOMINIQUE: Oh my god.

JOHN pulls out a ring.

DOMINIQUE: Fucking hell.

JOHN: This is what I have been trying to ask you all night. Marry me.

DANNY: Marry you? This guy really is fucking crazy.

DOMINIQUE: Danny. Please.

JOHN: "Danny, Danny, Danny". FUCK DANNY.

DOMINIQUE gets up in JOHN's face.

DOMINIQUE: John! Language!

JOHN: FUCK DANNY. I'm here now, Dominique.

JOHN grabs DOMINIQUE by the face and then suddenly shocked by his actions he lets go.

JOHN: Oh my god, Dominique. I'm sorry, Dominique. *(JOHN backs away)* That was because of how I feel... how you make me feel... how you feel too. I understand why you're doing this. You're scared.

DOMINIQUE: Do not fuck with me today, John.

DANNY: Scared of what?

JOHN: I love you Dominique and you're scared because you love me too.

DOMINIQUE: No.

JOHN: It's okay that this is all coming out, Dominique. This is good. This is what I've been waiting for. Thank you, Dominique. Thank you.

DANNY: Get away from him Dominique or I'll be out there. I'm tellin' ya.

DOMINIQUE starts to hyperventilate.

DOMINIQUE: I don't feel very well.

DOMINIQUE tries to stop herself from vomiting, hand over mouth, she scrambles towards the bathroom.

JOHN: Yes Dominique. Let all of it out. You'll feel better. We both will.

DOMINIQUE enters the bathroom. JOHN follows her in.

DANNY: Dominique???!!!???

DOMINIQUE: Danny???!!!???

DOMINIQUE heads straight to the toilet and is violently sick into it. Her body hunched up and convulsing as she clings to the bowl for security. JOHN is now in the bath-room too, standing above DOMINIQUE.

JOHN: Oh god.

JOHN goes to help DOMINIQUE. DANNY jumps up, stand-ing in the bath now.

DANNY: Get him outta here!

DOMINIQUE: Danny, it's fine.

JOHN: Oh for fuck's sake. 'Danny'? Still?

DOMINIQUE: *(To JOHN)* Yes! Danny! My Danny!

JOHN: Enough, Dominique! I'm your boyfriend now.

DANNY: Boyfriend?

JOHN: Look at me. I'm here now.

DOMINIQUE: No.

DANNY: Get him out Dominique. Get him out.

DOMINIQUE: *(To DANNY)* I can't Danny. I can't.

JOHN: This is crazy Dominique. You're losing it and I've had enough. I have a friend who can help you, a counsellor. It's the drugs Dominique. You need to get off them and you need grief counselling.

DANNY: Grief counselling? Dominique?

JOHN: Yes, grief counselling Dominique. I have a friend who can help there too. I'm trying to help you but you don't want to let me.

DOMINIQUE: *(To JOHN)* I don't need your help! I need Danny!

JOHN: Dominique! Danny is dead! He's dead!

DANNY: Dead? What the fuck? This geezer is mental.

JOHN: He's been dead for eighteen months.

DANNY: He's fucking lost it.

JOHN: How much longer is this going to go on for Domi

nique? How much more of this do you expect me to take?

DANNY: *(To DOMINIQUE)* Tell him Dominique. Tell him I'm not. Tell him the truth.

DOMINIQUE is violently sick in the toilet again, her body limp and lifeless now, flat on the floor, clinging to the base of the toilet.

JOHN: I'm sorry Dominique. I really didn't want it to be like this.

JOHN leaves the bathroom and sits down on the bed. DANNY is in shock.

DANNY: I ain't fucking dead. Tell him Dominique. Tell me.

DOMINIQUE crawls over to DANNY to comfort him. She clings to his body.

DOMINIQUE: Everything is fine Danny and I can make it even better. Do you want me to do that Danny? Look at me Danny, in the eye Danny.

DANNY: I don't understand. Tell me what happened.

DOMINIQUE: Nothing's happened. I've got your surprise Danny. Remember Danny? You got a surprise Danny.

DANNY: I think I just bloody had it.

DOMINIQUE steps back from DANNY.

DOMINIQUE: Well we don't have to babe. We can always cancel it babe.

DANNY: No! Don't do that, babe. Enough's been taken from me. I want it. What is it?

DOMINIQUE: Well, it's something that you don't have any more that I'm going to give back to ya.

A beat. DANNY thinks.

DANNY: My sanity babe?

DOMINIQUE: No babe. One step at a time babe. Happy Christmas babe.

DANNY: Christmas babe?

DOMINIQUE: Christmas babe.

DANNY: But it's only just October babe.

DOMINIQUE: Outside it is babe but inside it's Christmas. I wanted to give you something special and what could be more special than Christmas? By the time I've finished with you, you will wish it was Christmas every day. Just like the song babe.

DANNY: What song?

DOMINIQUE: 'I Wish it Could Be Christmas Every Day', babe.

DANNY: I don't know it.

DOMINIQUE: How can you not know it? They play it every year.

DANNY: I musta blocked it out. I ain't the biggest fan of Christmas.

DOMINIQUE: Awwww, I know you ain't but you ain't never had a Christmas with me, babe. Happy Christmas, Danny.

DANNY: Happy Christmas, Dominique.

DOMINIQUE pulls out a cracker.

DOMINIQUE: Wanna pull a cracker?

DANNY: I think I already have.

They pull the cracker. DANNY wears the paper crown.

DOMINIQUE: How can you not know that song?

DANNY shrugs.

DOMINIQUE: I love Christmas songs. 'Merry Christmas War is Over', 'Fairytale of New York'.

DANNY shakes his head.

DOMINIQUE: Bloody hell. 'Jingle Bells'? 'Silent Night'?

DANNY shakes his head again.

DOMINIQUE: I mean, help a girl out here.

DANNY: Kylie and Jason, 'Especially For You'.

DOMINIQUE: That not a Christmas song, babe.

DANNY: It was a hit over Christmas 1988. That makes it a Christmas song in my book. The only Christmas I can remember. 1988. The year my dad left *(DANNY starts to recite the 'Especially For You' song lyrics, as if it is a sonnet penned by William Shakespeare)*...'Especially for you...'

DOMINIQUE: '...I wanna let you know what I was going through...'

DANNY: '...All the time we were apart I thought of...'

DANNY / DOMINIQUE: '...You... You were in my heart... my love never changed... I still feel the same'.

DANNY: It's a song of loss, longing and desperation babe.

DOMINIQUE: Exactly babe, could suit any day of the year but I'll give it to ya 'cause it's your special day, okay.

DANNY: Okay. So now what?

DOMINIQUE: Christmas dinner.

DANNY: Wow.

DOMINIQUE: I know, right. Been a while ain't it babe? Come on babe.

DOMINIQUE starts to head out of the bathroom.

DANNY: Can't we eat in here?

DOMINIQUE: In the bath?

DANNY: Yeah?

DOMINIQUE: Can we not eat at the table like a normal family? Oh I give up but only because it's your special day but don't blame me when ya sprouts go soggy.

DOMINIQUE heads out of the bathroom. JOHN is still sitting on the bed.

DOMINIQUE: Alright darling. I'm just off to the kitchen. Gonna rustle us up a little something to eat.

DOMINIQUE heads off to the kitchen. JOHN shouts across to her.

JOHN: So you're just going to carry on? As 'normal'?

DOMINIQUE: It's what I do best darling. (*DOMINIQUE returns from the kitchen*) Nice day at work darling? See. (*Smiling, hand on hip, a Domestic Goddess*) Normal.

JOHN: We lost another one today. We're trained of course... in how to deal with it but that doesn't make it any easier...doesn't make them any less of a real person... doesn't make their family or the news I have for them any less real. Her name was Rachel, from Islington, on her way to see her boyfriend. She stepped out to cross the road and there was a bus and a motor cycle came up the side of it. I wish I didn't always remember the details but I do. All of them, logged away, in here

(JOHN points to his head) I think she must have been very pretty. I'm sorry. I'm being morbid again.

The microwave pings.

DOMINIQUE: Excuse me John.

DOMINIQUE heads back to the kitchen. JOHN continues to speak through the wall to DOMINIQUE.

JOHN: You know what's worse? When there's no one waiting outside for them... no one at home... no one else in the world; when they exist just on their own. I was like that before you. I didn't think this would ever happen to me. I thought this was just for other people, something only other people did or felt or had. You know, every day in the corridor at work... at the hospital or any evening on the walk home... in the street... any person who passed me, I'd look right into their eyes... daring them to connect. No one ever did. Until you.

DOMINIQUE returns with two microwave meals in her hands.

JOHN: Like that first time you felt me looking at you and you turned around to answer me, to see me. But now each day when we look into each others' eyes I see a piece of you disappear, and I worry that one day I won't be able to find you as there'll be nothing left and you'll be another one who can't see me.

DOMINIQUE: I'll always see ya John. Really. I'm good like that.

JOHN: I see you too Dominique. Even when we're apart.

DOMINIQUE: Bloody hell, I hope you ain't never caught me with no slap on.

DANNY: Wouldn't matter if he did!

JOHN: I see it all and it's killing me. It seems to be every where; people being swallowed, losing part of or all of who they are, sometimes ceasing to exist at all. I should be used to it by now, from work, but no, I'm not. Maybe I've logged too much away and my system is at collapse. I may malfunction. I'm sorry. I must be tired. Yes. I'm just so very tired.

DOMINIQUE: You just gotta hide from it all John. It's easy when you know how.

JOHN: I've tried but it always finds me. Yes, let's eat. God, I bloody reek of that hospital. I can't stand the smell. Just like everyone else. Who would have thought? I'll be telling you I can't stand the sight of blood next *(JOHN gets up)* Right. I'll freshen up in the kitchen sink. I know you don't like me to use the bathroom. *(JOHN goes as if he is about to head to the kitchen. He stops and looks at DOMINIQUE, then refers to the ready meals)* That's not for me, is it?

JOHN sinks back down on the bed. DOMINIQUE heads off to the bathroom door. When she reaches it she stands there for a moment with her back to JOHN.

DOMINIQUE: I'm sorry John.

JOHN lies down on the bed now, weeping as he does so. After a moment DOMINIQUE puts down the meals, goes over to the bed and then covers JOHN with the duvet. She stands above him as JOHN melts, breaks down and melts further away. DOMINIQUE then turns away and heads back into the bathroom to DANNY.

DOMINIQUE: Dinner is served babe!

DANNY: Yeah baby!

DOMINIQUE: I hope you're hungry babe 'cause I have been slaving over a tepid to cool microwave for you. Hold these babe.

DOMINIQUE passes DANNY one ready meal.

DOMINIQUE: Potatoes.

DANNY: Lovely babe.

DOMINIQUE: And veg.

DOMINIQUE passes DANNY the second container. DANNY is about to tuck in.

DOMINIQUE: Wait. I gotta get the gravy.

DOMINIQUE heads off to the kitchen.

DANNY: Gravy? For the turkey? Oh yeah. I remember now. Result!

DOMINIQUE stops in her tracks.

DOMINIQUE: Sorry babe?

DANNY: You said you're getting the gravy babe and I said for the turkey babe.

DOMINIQUE: Turkey babe?

DANNY: Yeah, turkey babe.

DOMINIQUE: Oh fucking hell Danny *(DOMINIQUE rushes back into the bathroom)* I've forgotten the bloody turkey. It ain't Christmas without a fucking turkey.

DANNY: Well that's alright Dominique.

DOMINIQUE: No it ain't alright Danny. I fucked up. Again. I try and do something nice and normal and I am evidently not made for either. Fuck. I can't even provide for my man.

DOMINIQUE sits down on the edge of the bath. DANNY goes to her and puts his arm around her.

DANNY: But babe, look at all this you cooked.

DOMINIQUE: It's hardly cooking is it Danny. I just pushed a few of the right buttons.

DANNY: And pushing all the right buttons is what you do best my darlin' and you provide plenty Dominique, don't you worry. Fuck normal. You're better than that. Fuck normal. And fuck nice too. You're nicer than nice.

DOMINIQUE: Nicer than nice am I Danny?

DANNY: Even nicer than that.

DOMINIQUE: I think you're nicer than nice too.

DANNY: Good. Cause I'm still here babe. Always will be. No matter what. Especially For You.

A moment.

DANNY: What happened to me Dominique?

DOMINIQUE: You ain't tried ya dinner yet.

A beat.

DOMINIQUE: It was our first and last Christmas or at least it shoulda been. After dinner I went out to get dessert, well… a tin of fruit salad… that's all they had in that shit-hole of a corner shop and I came back with it and there you were… in the bath… as you always were… as you will always will be. Carrier bag over your head. The carrier bag I'd brought that bloody Christmas dinner home in. You hadn't slept for days. You'd lost it. Maybe the voice in the wall told you to do it. Your dad getting his own back. *(Beat)* These fucking walls. Remember what we used to say Danny? "If these walls could talk". I guess eventually they did. We tried to revive you. We got you down the hospital but it was too late. John was a consultant on duty that night. I met him when I was queuing at the vending machine for an hot chocolate…

Flashback

DOMINIQUE at the vending machine. She puts some

change in to pay for her hot drink. Her change is immediately swallowed with no drink in return. DOMINIQUE hits the vending machine in frustration and fury.

JOHN: May I help you with that?

DOMINIQUE: The bastard machines gobbled me money. I just want me Mocha Choco Chino Surprise.

JOHN: Here.

JOHN puts some change into the vending machine which delivers. JOHN hands DOMINIQUE her Mocha Choco Chino Surprise.

DOMINIQUE: Thank you. What a gentleman.

JOHN: Some of us still exist.

DOMINIQUE: And some of ya don't.

JOHN: I know. I'm sorry about your...

DOMINIQUE *(Interrupting)*: ....'bout my Danny? That makes two of us.

JOHN: I was just about to sneak out to the courtyard for a quick fag. Care to join me?

DOMINIQUE: Smoking's bad for you.

JOHN: I know. Well, perhaps you'd like to accompany me to enjoy the view.

DOMINIQUE: Whitechapel High Street?

JOHN: It's what you make of it. Like everything else.

DOMINIQUE smiles at JOHN.

DOMINIQUE: I'll just get me handbag. I've got a bottle of Baileys in it to go with this.

JOHN: Sneaking in the miniatures aren't we?

DOMINIQUE: Oh no. I don't do miniatures, doctor....?

DOMINIQUE looks for a name badge.

JOHN: John. My name's John.

DOMINIQUE: And my name's...

JOHN *(Interrupting)*: Dominique.

Present day.

DOMINIQUE: ...and John was comforting and kind, and in this city...

DANNY *(Interrupting – he understands)*: ...in this world. It's hard to find. How did I let this happen? How did I get here? So far gone. Fuck. When I think back to bein' a kid. This weren't what my Mum and Dad had planned for me. I've let 'em down...

DOMINIQUE: No Danny no...

DANNY: Yes. What would they have said if they coulda seen me in this bath with a fucking carrier bag over my head!

DOMINIQUE: Danny, stop please.

DANNY: I was gonna take you back home, for me mum's roast dinner. You were gonna take me clubbing down Vauxhall, my old stomping ground. We were even gonna go down the pub, The Royston Arms. But none of it. We can't do none of it anymore.

DOMINIQUE: Danny we can. We're doing it now. The club is right here. The pub is too. I can even taste your mum's cooking. All of it... here... as many times as we like. Don't have to be our first or last Christmas. Can't ya see? If we want, it really can be Christmas every day.

DANNY: No. Just you and me left now girl. Wow. Look at all this. (DANNY goes to DOMINIQUE's make up) Like sweets. All them colours and flavours. This is you. Gonna inhale you. Get high off you.

DANNY starts to go through DOMINIQUE's make up. DANNY finds some glitzy make up, sprinkles it into his crack pipe and starts to smoke.

DANNY: Mmmmmmmm.

DOMINIQUE: How do I taste?

DANNY: Colourful.

DOMINIQUE: I wanna try me.

DOMINIQUE grabs the pipe, DANNY lights it for her, DOMINIQUE smokes.

DANNY: What about yours?

DOMINIQUE: My what?

DANNY: Your mum and dad. Where are they now?

DOMINIQUE: They're gone too. *(DOMINIQUE smokes some more)* I'm an orphan. Like you. See? We really was meant to be.

DANNY: What happened to them?

DOMINIQUE: Who knows. Here one day and then gone the next. Blown off the edge off a cliff by an over-eager gust of wind? Trampled to death by a runaway herd of horses, or maybe just sucked into a parallel universe somewhere and someplace better than here with me. Could be any of those reasons or any other equally viable option. *(DOMINIQUE sucks on the pipe again)* But wow... I taste good. I want some more of me. *(DOMINIQUE goes to smoke again).*

DANNY: You're addictive. *(DANNY goes to grab the pipe)* My turn again.

DOMINIQUE: I ain't finished with me yet.

DOMINIQUE goes to suck on the pipe again.

DANNY: Yes you are. *(DANNY grabs the pipe off her)* C'mon

Dominique. You're my desert. I didn't get to have it last time did I?

DOMINIQUE: The fruit salad? No, ya didn't did ya…

DANNY: 'Cause you went out to get it and when ya came back I was…

DOMINIQUE: I know what you were Danny. I found ya. I don't need reminding.

DANNY: I'm sorry Dominique. *(A beat, then sarcastic)* It must be really tough for you, Dominique, that my life is over… that I ain't here no more. Life's a bitch, innit, Dominique.

DOMINIQUE: No. Not tough for me. For you. I don't care about me. I care about you.

DANNY: Least you can do considering I'm dead from your dinner.

DOMINIQUE: From my dinner?

DANNY: Yeah. You brought it in here, in the carrier bag, the one I put over my head. No dinner, no carrier bag. No carrier bag, no dead Danny.

DOMINIQUE: I went shopping for *you.* To do something nice for *you* 'cause of your dad.

DANNY: You leave my family out of this!

DOMINIQUE: And if it hadn't been the bag you'd of found

something else. I only made the dinner 'cause your old man fucked up all your Christmases. If anyone did it... he did it... yeah... your own dad did it.

DANNY: I told you, Dominique. Don't talk about him like that. (Suddenly aware of the walls again) He'll hear ya!

DOMINIQUE: He killed ya 'cause he was a fuck up like you. Thank fuck you can't get me up the duff or I'd give birth to a fuck up as well and I'd have to get the fucking doctor to shove it back in.

DANNY: You'd be lucky love. You ain't got the right equipment to pop one out never mind shove one back in. I'll show you a fuck up. I'll show you how it really goes.

DANNY pulls out the carrier bag.

DOMINIQUE: No Danny. Put that away.

DANNY is manic, wired and aggressive.

DANNY: Just showing you what you missed. You only found me. You weren't here to see it, to stop me... to save me. (Enjoying himself now, like a ringmaster in a circus) This is what really happened, Dominique. Yeah. Look closely, Dominique. You'll like this one, Dominique.

DANNY starts to pull the carrier bag over his head.

DOMINIQUE: No Danny. Don't do it!!!

DANNY: Don't tell me you didn't wonder, Dominique. How I did it? How long it took? What I looked like the moment

I stopped breathing?

DOMINIQUE: Oh god Danny, please.

DANNY: They always say 'he looked so peaceful' when they see a body laid out but not me. I'm not peaceful and I'm not laid out. Lemme tell ya what ya missed. One, my breathing, regular at first then quick and fast like stabs in the dark. Two, my pretty blues eyes poppin' outta their sockets and then three, my innocent, young face slowly turnin' purple. I was proper fucked, more fucked than I'd ever been and this weren't no good night out either. I was indoors. In here. Alone. Without you cause you left me cause you knew what I was 'bout to do!

DOMINIQUE: No I didn't Danny. How could I possibly have known?

DANNY: You didn't wanna be here when it happened. For when I called your name. Dominique! *(DANNY grabs DOMINIQUE and shakes her each time he says her name, each shout more desperate than the last)* Dominique! Dominique! You weren't here for that amazing moment I realised it was really gonna happen… that moment when I let the last of my life get sucked outta me… and you weren't here the moment I changed my mind… when I decided I didn't wanna top myself… and you weren't here for the moment when I realised it was too late. You weren't here for none of it and it's your fault I'm stuck here Dominique and I ain't never gonna let you forget it.

DOMINIQUE: Oh god Danny, no!

DOMINIQUE runs out of the bathroom and wakes JOHN

65

up.

DOMINIQUE: John! Please! He's going to do it again! You're a doctor. Do something.

JOHN: Do what?

DOMINIQUE: He's gonna kill himself! Again! To show me!

JOHN: Oh bloody hell.

DOMINIQUE has by now pulled JOHN into the bathroom.

DANNY: What the fuck is he doing in here?

JOHN: Oh bloody hell.

DANNY: I'll show ya both then! Lover Boy too!

DOMINIQUE: He can't see ya Danny!

DANNY: No, but he'll see you and that'll be enough. Your face'll tell him all he needs to know.

DOMINIQUE: No Danny. Don't do this to us. Not again.

DANNY: Are ya ready? *(DANNY starts to adjust the plastic bag on his head)* One… two…

DOMINIQUE: Danny! Please don't make me remember you like this.

JOHN: Where is he, Dominique?

DOMINIQUE points at DANNY. JOHN speaks to the general area where DOMINIQUE pointed.

JOHN: Danny. It's me John.

DANNY: I know who you bloody are mate.

DOMINIQUE: *(To JOHN, incredulous that he is speaking to DANNY)* You see him?

JOHN: I... feel him, Dominique. Now I know we haven't always seen eye to eye Danny...

DANNY: Nah but you're gonna see this... or at least she is.

DANNY goes to pull the carrier bag fully over his head. DOMINIQUE runs to JOHN and buries her head in his chest.

DOMINIQUE: John, make him stop!

JOHN: Danny! Look at Dominique. Do you really want to do this to the woman you love? Do you want to break her completely?

DANNY: Why should I be the only one that's broken?

JOHN: What does he say Dominique?

DOMINIQUE: He says why should he be the only one that's...

JOHN: *(Interrupting and to DANNY)* ...we're all broken, Danny.

DOMINIQUE: *(To JOHN)* You hear him too?

DANNY: Yeah well I'm dead. Top that dickhead.

DOMINIQUE: *(To JOHN)* And he's saying that you're a...

JOHN: *(Interrupting)* Yes, thank you Dominique. I'm terribly sorry for your loss Danny. This is all very nasty business.

DANNY: Then why can't she feel it like I do?

JOHN: She does feel it Danny. We all do. I can help you... both of you... all three of us. I can make this better. I can make us strong. *(To DOMINIQUE)* I could be Danny and you could be you. I could be in the bath and something could go wrong but you could save me and bring me back and that'll make everything good and special and clean. You'd of been there when it happened Dominique and so there'll be... a resolution. *(To DOMINIQUE and DANNY)* For all of us *(To DOMINIQUE)* because you'll have been able to save me. *(To DOMINIQUE and DANNY)* We'd have been able to save all of us. *(To DOMINIQUE)* Please just let us save ourselves Dominique. Give that to me. To us. Make it feel good again. Would you do that Dominique? Please Dominique.

DOMINIQUE: No.

DANNY: Do it Dominique. You'll be doing that for us.

JOHN: Anything you could do would help, Dominique. Even if it's just for a moment, it's better than nothing.

DOMINIQUE: I can't.

DANNY: Yes ya can. It'll be different this time.

DOMINIQUE: How?

JOHN: We'll be together. This time it'll be for all of us.

The landline rings.

DANNY *(To DOMINIQUE)*: You should speak to them.

DOMINIQUE: Speak to who?

DANNY: Your mum and dad, Dominique. That's who's calling.

DOMINIQUE: No. Can't be. My mum and dad are dead.

JOHN: Alive, Dominique. They're alive.

DANNY: They call here all the time. I used to answer but then I stopped. They couldn't hear me when I spoke anyways... but I could hear them. I thought it was a wrong number at first because they kept asking for...

DOMINIQUE *(Interrupting)*: No one here by that name. Not anymore.

JOHN: They love you Dominique.

DANNY: He's right. That's why they're calling here.

DOMINIQUE: They left me. Like everyone does.

DANNY / JOHN: I'm still here Dominique.

DANNY: Go on Dominique. Answer it or else I will.

DOMINIQUE: Do it. They won't hear you anyway.

JOHN: You should take that call Dominique. You came from them.

DOMINIQUE: No. I came from myself.

JOHN: Not to start with darling.

DOMINIQUE goes to rush out the bathroom to answer the phone but she can't move. She is frozen.

DOMINIQUE: I wanna but I can't.

The phone stops ringing. DOMINIQUE is defeated.

DOMINIQUE: I was just a little *(DOMINQUE tries to say 'boy' but it gets stuck in her throat)* and it was just a Wednesday and I know it was just a Wednesday because we had a different meal for each evening of the week, seven of 'em rotating; my mother liked her routine and Wednesday was Alpha Bite day, those crispy letters shaped out of potatoes, and my mother would serve them up with baked beans and sausages to cover the other essential food groups, and round the side of my plate, with my Alpha Bites, she would spell out my name, my birth name which was *(DOMINIQUE goes to say her birth name but it gets lodged in her throat)* and one Wednesday evening, when my Alpha Bites were ready, Mother called me down, by my birth name of course, which was *(DOMINIQUE tries to say again, but again, it won't come out)* but I was too busy hurting myself here *(DOMINIQUE*

70

indicates to one forearm) and here *(and then the other forearm)* with a fucking Action Man doll that I got given too but I'd PULLED MINE'S HEAD OFF and CHEWED ROUND THE EDGE OF ITS NECK to make it nice and sharp and I'd STICK IT IN ME HERE *(DOMINIQUE demonstrates on one forearm)* and I'd do THE SAME HERE *(DOMIN-IQUE demonstrates on her other forearm)* and I did it every night, over and over, because I liked my routine too, and that Wednesday I did it so bad and so good that I bled all the way downstairs, into the kitchen, up onto the kitchen table, where the spelt-out Alpha Bites were waiting for me, my blood whooshing all over 'em like an angry red sea lapping at the shore, till those fucking Alpha Bites were washed away and that little *(DOMINIQUE tries to say 'boy' again)* was washed away with them too and 'that' name was never said, nor seen nor spelt out of reconstituted potato ever again, and that was the day that Dominique was born and one morning, one year later to the exact day itself, I went downstairs and there on the kitchen table, with mother and father sitting either side of it, was a ginormous sponge and cream and jam birthday cake covered in cavity-inducing neon pink icing, all shaped like a great big fuck off letter 'D', and there were party hats and a birthday banner too; draped across the chimney breast, 'Happy Birthday Dominique'. Mother and Father were in shock: I'd sneaked down in the middle of the night, set the room and table and baked me own cake too. I always fucking hated pink, I still don't know why I chose it, it was a moment of attempted heteronormative assimilation, don't judge me – and that was the beginning and also the end. I went out that morning to buy myself a better toy and Mother and Father never saw Dominique again.

71

DANNY: How did they find you here, babe? How did they get the number?

DOMINIQUE: 'Cause I'd phone from this number and hang up when they answered.

DOMINIQUE turns to JOHN.

DOMINIQUE: You'll need a safe word John.

JOHN: A safe word?

DOMINIQUE: In case something goes wrong. Everyone should have a safe word. Whaddaya want yours to be?

JOHN: Oh god. I don't know. A safe word. Oh god.
DOMINIQUE: The name of your first pet? The street where you grew up? Your mother's maiden name?

JOHN: Love. I want my safe word to be love.

DOMINIQUE: Well you've chosen the most unsafe word in the English dictionary but the customer is always right.

DANNY: Love it is.

JOHN: Love it is.

With DANNY's help JOHN gets into the bath. DANNY gets in after him, sitting behind JOHN. DANNY passes JOHN the plastic bag.

JOHN: It's okay Dominique. I safe word you.

JOHN puts the plastic bag over his head. DOMINIQUE immediately plunges JOHN's head under the water.

JOHN quickly comes back up.

JOHN: I want you to show me you safe word me.

DOMINIQUE immediately plunges JOHN's head back under. After a short moment JOHN resurfaces again.

JOHN: More. Show me how much. Like it was for Danny. Show me how much you safe word him.

DOMINIQUE pushes JOHN back under the water, this time with more force. JOHN comes up again gasping for air. DOMINIQUE gasping for air too, exhausted.
DANNY: Are you alright babe?

DOMINIQUE: I can't go on Danny.

DANNY: I'll help.

DANNY places his hands on top of Dominque's and joins her in plunging JOHN's head underwater. After a moment of holding JOHN's head under:

DOMINIQUE: Okay Danny that's enough.

DANNY: He wanted to know what it was like. How we safe word each other. How you safe word him.

JOHN comes up.

JOHN: Safe word!

DOMINIQUE: There. He's said it.

DANNY: He ain't said it properly.

DANNY plunges JOHN's head back underwater.

DOMINIQUE: He just did.

DANNY: You can say it for him if you like babe.

DOMINIQUE: Me?

DANNY: Yeah. You. Safe word. Say it. If you ain't too scared.

DOMINIQUE: Scared? Okay. Safe word! See Danny. I said it.
DANNY continues to hold JOHN under.

DOMINIQUE: Danny! I said it!

DANNY: No you ain't. Not properly.

DOMINIQUE frees herself and backs away from the bath.

DOMINIQUE: Safe word! Safe word! Safe word! See, Danny,
I'm saying it Danny.

DANNY: SAY IT PROPERLY DOMINIQUE! PLEASE! STOP ME!
DOMINIQUE! PLEASE!

DOMINIQUE: I can't Danny. I can't.

*DOMINIQUE runs back to the bath and tries to pull
DANNY away from JOHN. DANNY pushes DOMINIQUE
off, sending her flying.*

DANNY: Please Dominique! Just say it! Please!

DOMINIQUE: Love Danny!

DANNY and JOHN die.

DOMINIQUE: Love. Love. Love.

DOMINIQUE runs over to DANNY and JOHN.

DOMINIQUE: John? Danny?

DOMINIQUE throws herself on top of DANNY and JOHN and then lets out a succession of screams from the pit of her stomach, pained and feral-like, sliding down onto the floor as she does so. After a moment, Dominique sits up properly and looks around her.

DOMINIQUE: I really need to stop having boyfriends. I don't seem to bring 'em that much luck. But we carry on, as normal. Someone needs to take control and as always it comes down to the bloody woman. Now Danny, you ain't touched your dinner and John you must be starving, you've been on a forty-eight hour shift. Now, I'm gonna pop back down that shop and get us a lovely bit of turkey to go with that dinner and then we can all be together... like a proper family and yes, like any family we have our ups and downs but like any family we just gotta look at what we've got because others would kill to have what we have. I'm lucky. I'm spoilt. I got ya both forever and I just knew you two would get on. John, every step on the stairs, every bunch of flowers, every time I save myself, it's you. You're with me. And Danny, every bath, every puff of smoke freeing itself into the air, every fuck-

75

ing Christmas dinner is you. It's all both of ya. Ya both with me. I ain't alone. My boys and I.

DOMINIQUE's mobile phone rings. She gets up to go and answer it but her legs give way and she falls to the floor. DOMINIQUE crawls through into the living area to answer her phone. She sits on the edge of the bed as we first saw her. She answers her mobile.

DOMINIQUE: *(Phone voice)* How may I be of assistance? ...and what exactly is it that you're after sweetheart? I offer a full unhurried service. Your pleasure is my pleasure. My measurements are.... sorry sweetheart? *(DOMINIQUE holds the mobile phone to her chest)* Oh come on sweetheart. Spit. It. Out.

The landline rings.

Lights.

Music: Kylie and Jason 'Especially For You'.

End.

Also available from Team Angelica Publishing

'Reasons to Live' by Rikki Beadle-Blair
'What I Learned Today' by Rikki Beadle-Blair

'Faggamuffin' by John R Gordon
'Colour Scheme' by John R Gordon
'Souljah' by John R Gordon

'Fairytales for Lost Children' by Diriye Osman

'Black & Gay in the UK – an anthology' edited by John R Gordon & Rikki Beadle-Blair

'Tiny Pieces of Skull' by Roz Kaveney